WOMEN EXPLORERS IN AFRICA

CHRISTINA DODWELL, DELIA AKELEY, MARY KINGSLEY, FLORENCE VON SASS- BAKER, ALEXANDRINE TINNE

by Margo McLoone

Reading Consultant
Dr. Patricia Gilmartin, Ph.D.
Professor of Geography
University of South Carolina

CAPSTONE PRESS
MANKATO, MINNESOTA

C A P S T O N E P R E S S
818 North Willow Street • Mankato, MN 56001

Printed in the United States of America.

Library of Congress Cataloging-in-Publication Data
McLoone, Margo.
    Women explorers in Africa: Christina Dodwell, Delia Akeley, Mary Kingsley, Florence von Sass-Baker, Alexandrine Tinne/by Margo McLoone.
    p. cm.
    Summary: Summarizes the lives and accomplishments of five women who were explorers in Africa.
    ISBN 1-56065-505-4
    1. Africa--Discovery and exploration--Juvenile literature.
2. Women explorers--Africa--Biography--Juvenile literature.
3. Explorers--Africa--Biography--Juvenile literature.
[1. Explorers. 2. Women--Biography. 3. Africa--Discovery and exploration.]
DT3.W64   1997
916.04'092'2--dc20
[B]
                                                    96-43334
                                                       CIP
                                                        AC

Photo credits
Carl Akeley, courtesy American Museum of Natural History, 14 (neg. 211208), 17 (neg. 211209)
Jean Buldain, 11, 18
FPG, 27
Paul Harris/Royal Geographic Society, London, 8
International/Grant, 33
Royal Geographic Society, London, 22, 28, 36
Unicorn, 34, 40, Reininger, 4; Shores, 6

TABLE OF CONTENTS

Chapter 1 What Is an Explorer?........................ 5

Chapter 2 Christina Dodwell............................ 9

Chapter 3 Delia Akeley.................................. 15

Chapter 4 Mary Kingsley................................ 23

Chapter 5 Florence von Sass-Baker 29

Chapter 6 Alexandrine Tinne 37

Chronology 42

Words to Know 44

To Learn More 45

Useful Addresses 46

Internet Sites 47

Index 48

CHAPTER 1

WHAT IS AN EXPLORER?

Explorers are people who want to learn about new and faraway places. They gather information about remote places and people. They usually write about their experiences, so others can learn.

Exploring versus Traveling

Explorers go places very few people have ever been. These lands are wild and sometimes dangerous. There are no buildings, hotels, or restaurants. There are also no roads. They must find or build their own paths.

Explorers travel in many ways. Sometimes they use camels or canoes.

Explorers in Africa must be careful of wild animals that roam the grasslands.

Traveling is different than exploring. Travelers usually go to places where there are other people. They stay in hotels and eat in restaurants. Travelers go places for pleasure.

Dangers Explorers Face

Explorers face many problems. The places they go are not on any maps. They use a compass. A compass tells them what direction they are going. But even with a compass, they can become lost.

Sometimes explorers climb high, icy mountains. Other explorers paddle down dangerous rivers. Often, they are attacked by wild animals. They cannot always find a hospital if they are hurt or sick.

Weather is also a danger. Blizzards, floods, or earthquakes can hurt explorers. It takes a long time for people to find and rescue a lost or injured explorer.

Women Explorers in Africa

When people think about explorers, they usually think of men. But many women have explored unknown lands. They have made important discoveries.

This book tells about the lives and experiences of five women explorers. They left their homes for adventure. These women explored the dangerous wilderness of Africa.

They explored places few people had been. Their experiences have helped people learn about the animals, land, and cultures in Africa.

CHAPTER 2

CHRISTINA DODWELL 1951—

Christina Dodwell was born on February 1, 1951, in Nigeria, Africa. Her parents were from England. The family moved back to London, England, when Dodwell was six years old.

When Dodwell grew older, she worked as an interior designer. She decorated the inside of buildings. She was used to life in London. But things were about to change.

Christina Dodwell was born in Nigeria, Africa.

Stranded in Africa

In 1975, Christina Dodwell, her friend Lesley Jamieson, and two men were on vacation in Africa. The group crossed the Sahara Desert together. After that, the two men stole the jeep. They left Dodwell and Jamieson behind.

The women were left in wild, unexplored land called the bush. They had no food. The only way they could travel was on foot.They walked until they found wild horses to ride.

After a week of searching for help, they found a village. The villagers fed them peanuts and corn. They also gave them yogurt made from milk, fresh animal blood, and urine.

Traveling through Africa

Dodwell decided not to go home. She stayed in Africa and had many exciting adventures. She traveled more than 20,000 miles (32,000 kilometers). Mostly, she traveled alone on horseback or by camel.

African villagers gave Dodwell food and water.

Once Dodwell bought a canoe. For seven weeks, she paddled down the Congo River. It was full of dangerous whirlpools. Whirlpools are masses of water that spin very fast. Hippos and crocodiles lived in the water.

Friendly villages were scattered along the banks of the river. She met many villagers who

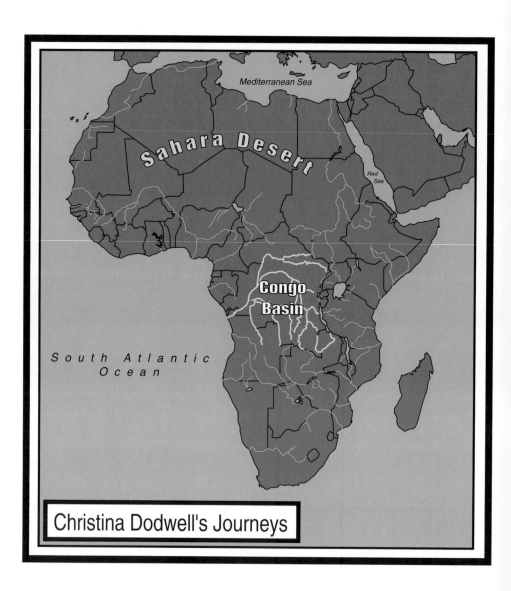

Mediterranean Sea

Sahara Desert

Red Sea

Congo Basin

South Atlantic Ocean

Christina Dodwell's Journeys

gave her food. They also gave her tips for traveling on the river.

Skills to Survive in the Bush

Dodwell learned many skills in Africa. She rode elephants and camels. She found water in the desert. She made soap from plants and brushed her teeth with twigs. She used herbs to heal wounds. She skinned crocodiles.

For food, Dodwell built an oven in the ground. She cooked everything from bread to wild hedgehogs.

In 1984, Dodwell wrote a book called *An Explorer's Handbook*. In the book, she tells what she learned from being deserted in Africa.

Beyond Africa

Dodwell eventually returned to England. But she still travels to remote regions of the world. Dodwell has explored for 15 years. She has traveled to China, Mexico, Pakistan, and Tibet.

CHAPTER 3

DELIA AKELEY
1875—1970

Delia Denning was born in Beaver Dam, Wisconsin, on December 5, 1875. She was the ninth child in the family. At the age of 13, she ran away from home and went to Milwaukee.

There she met Carl Akeley. He was a taxidermist at the Milwaukee Public Musuem. A taxidermist stuffs animal skins to put them on display.

Delia married Carl in 1902. They traveled to Africa in 1905 to collect African elephants for a museum display. The Akeleys killed the animals, then collected and preserved their

Delia Akeley collected animal samples for museums.

skins. Once back at the museum, they stuffed the animals' skins and put them on display.

Safari across Africa

Delia Akeley led an expedition into Africa in 1924. She was the first woman hired to collect wildlife samples for the Brooklyn Museum in New York.

She was also the first woman to lead a safari. A safari is a trip organized for hunting or exploring, usually in Africa.

It was Akeley's third trip to Africa. On other trips, she had gone with her husband, Carl. But they were divorced. Akeley went to Africa without Carl.

While on safari, Akeley traveled through rivers, deserts, and jungles. She found the hidden home of the Bambute (bam-BOO-tee) tribe. The Bambute are Pygmies (PIG-mees). Pygmies are people who live near the African equator. Their height ranges between four and five feet (1 and 1-1/2 meters).

Delia Akeley was the first woman to lead a safari.

Living with the Bambute

The Bambute were surprised when Akeley
found them. She was the first outsider to visit
their village. She was a 49-year-old woman
with white skin and white hair.

Her hair shocked them. Their hair did not
turn white until they were close to death. The

Akeley hunted elephants with the Bambute tribe.

Bambute called her the woman with an old head on a young body.

For three months, Akeley lived and hunted with the Bambute. She learned a lot about the Pygmy people. They ate caterpillars, lizards, and roots. The men hunted monkeys, birds, and elephants.

18

Elephant Hunt

The Bambute took Akeley on an elephant hunt with them. The hunters thought her clothes made too much noise. They wanted her to hunt naked like they did. She refused.

When the Bambute finished eating the elephant, they crawled inside its skin to sleep. Akeley was left alone to keep the fire going. She wanted help. So she told them she saw a leopard. Several men came out of the elephant to help her keep guard.

Akeley wanted to share something she knew, too. She taught the Bambute children how to jump rope using forest vines.

Cannibal Feast

After Akeley left the Bambute, she continued to travel in the Congo. She stayed in a village of cannibals. Cannibals are people who eat human flesh.

One evening, two men came to her door and dropped off a steaming pot and a bundle wrapped in banana

Ivory

Elephant tusks are made of ivory. The largest tusk found weighed 236 pounds (107 kilograms).

Poachers are hunters who kill elephants for their ivory tusks. In 1989, elephants were put on the endangered species list. It is now against the law for people to buy or sell elephant ivory.

19

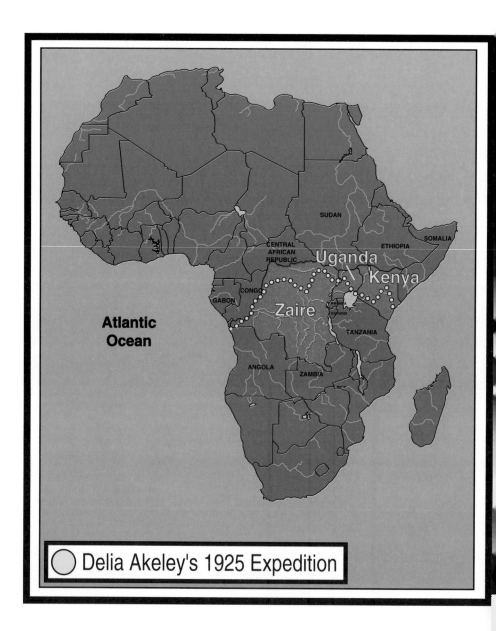

Atlantic Ocean

SUDAN
SOMALIA
CENTRAL AFRICAN REPUBLIC
ETHIOPIA
Uganda
Kenya
CONGO
GABON
RWANDA
BURUNDI
Zaire
TANZANIA
ANGOLA
ZAMBIA

Delia Akeley's 1925 Expedition

leaves. It was food from the leader of the village. Akeley went closer to look into the steaming pot.

One of the men lifted up a well-cooked human forearm. He then picked up a cooked hand. Akeley decided not to eat the food. Two of her African servants ate the cannibal feast.

Akeley continued to cross Africa. She became the first Western woman to cross Africa from the Indian Ocean to the Atlantic Ocean alone.

Out of Africa

Akeley was a member of the Society of Woman Geographers, which is based in Washington, D.C. She wrote two books and gave talks about her experiences in Africa. The African animal samples that she collected are in museums around the United States.

Akeley married Dr. Warren Howe and retired from exploring in 1939. She died in Florida in 1970.

CHAPTER 4

MARY KINGSLEY
1862—1900

Mary Kingsley was born in London, England, on October 13, 1862. Her father, George Kingsley, spent most of his life traveling around the world.

When Mary was 26, her mother became so sick that she was unable to get out of bed. For four years, Mary took care of her mother 24 hours a day.

Mary's parents spent a lot of money to educate her brother, Charles. They spent no money on her education. She stayed home with her mother. She read many books.

Mary Kingsley nursed her mother 24 hours a day.

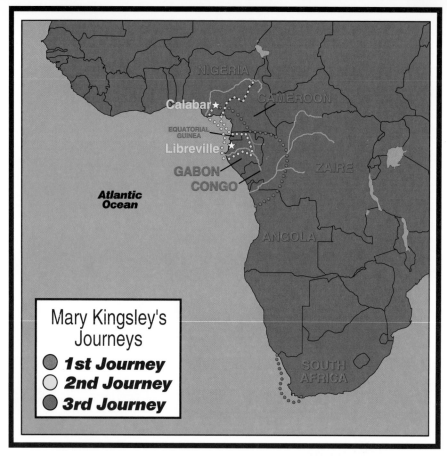

Mary Kingsley's
Journeys
⬤ 1st Journey
◯ 2nd Journey
⬤ 3rd Journey

Both of her parents died when Mary was 30 years old. Charles left to travel in Asia. Mary felt alone and sad. But she was also free. She could travel, too.

To West Africa

In 1893, Kingsley took a cargo boat to West Africa. She was interested in nature. She wanted to search for rare African fish and insects. She also wanted to learn about native religions and customs.

Kingsley traveled the streams and swamps of West Africa. She collected samples of fish for museums. She traded fishhooks, cloth, and tobacco for supplies. She learned about African religions and art.

After nine months of exploring, Kingsley returned to England. But she had fallen in love with Africa, its people, and the excitement of travel.

Back to Africa

Kingsley returned to Africa in 1895. She traveled unmapped country to collect fish for the British Museum. She explored the Ogowe River.

She journeyed among the Fang people. The Fang people were cannibals. She traded things for African masks and musical instruments.

Kingsley always wore a long, puffy, black skirt, and a black head covering. She carried a parasol. A parasol is a small umbrella used to protect the head from sun. She also carried a black bag, a box for collecting fish, and a suitcase in a waterproof bag. She had a gun and knife hidden in her clothes for protection.

Wild Times

Kingsley wrote letters about her wild times in Africa. Once, she fell into a deep hunter's trap. Ebony stakes pointed up from the bottom of the pit. Her puffy skirt saved her from being spiked to death.

Another time, she was alone on a small island and came face-to-face with an angry hippo. She chased him away by poking him with her parasol.

In the swamps, a crocodile suddenly leaped up and put its two front feet on her canoe. She used her paddle to knock the crocodile on the snout. He swam away.

One time, Kingsley was a guest in a remote Fang village. Nasty smells came from some small, hanging bags in her hut. When she opened the bags, they contained human ears, eyes, toes, and a hand. The owner of the hut had kept these as souvenirs from a cannibal dinner.

A crocodile attacked Mary Kingsley's canoe.

Understanding Africa

Kingsley's nature collection was donated to England's Royal Botanical Garden. She wrote two books, *Travels in West Africa* and *West African Studies*. The books helped people in Europe understand African people.

Kingsley went back to Africa in 1900. The Boer War was being fought. She went to a South African hospital in Simonstown and nursed prisoners. While there, she caught a fever and died. She was 38 years old.

Lady Baker

FLORENCE VON SASS-BAKER 1841—1916

Florence von Sass was born in the mountains of Transylvania, Romania, in 1841. Most of her childhood is a mystery. Her family was murdered in the Hungarian Revolution of 1848.

Von Sass escaped. She was hidden by a family of servants. For 10 years, no one knew where von Sass was. Then she was seen in Widdin, Bulgaria, in 1858. She had been captured and was being sold by Turkish slave traders.

Florence von Sass was forced to work as a slave.

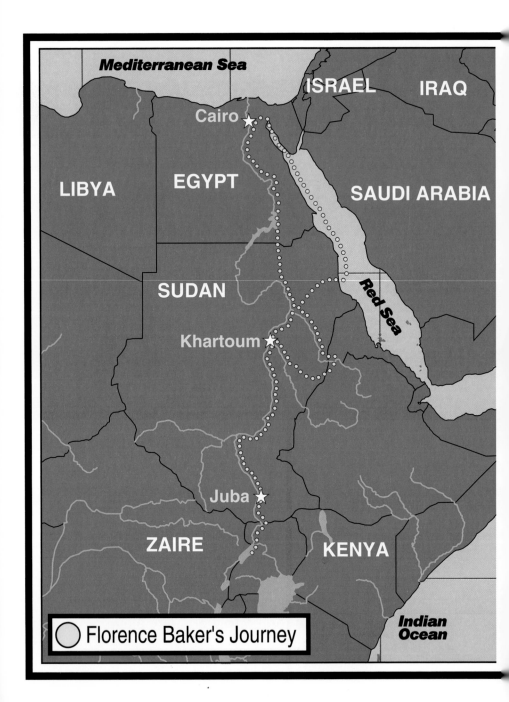

Florence Baker's Journey

From Slave to Explorer

Samuel Baker was a wealthy Englishman on vacation in Bulgaria. Baker was disgusted with the slave trade. He saw von Sass being sold as a slave and bought her freedom.

They fell in love and were married. Von Sass-Baker was 18 years old. Samuel was 38. Together, they decided to explore Africa.

The Mystery of the River Nile

In the 1800s, the Nile was a mystery. No one knew where the great river began. Many people tried to find its source.

Explorers traveled far into the center of Africa to search. The Bakers joined the race to find the source of the Nile.

Adventures on the River Nile

The Bakers put together an expedition. An expedition is a trip taken by a group of people for a special purpose. The Bakers sailed from Cairo, Egypt, down the Nile on April 15, 1861.

For the next four years, they sailed on the Nile. They crossed deserts. They walked

through steamy jungles. They survived heatstroke, brain fever, and malaria. Malaria is a dangerous tropical disease.

Von Sass-Baker made clothing from native cloth and animal skins. She learned how to shoot a rifle. When they were attacked by local armies, she fought back. Once, she saved Baker's life. She shot a charging rhinoceros when his gun failed.

Disappointment

The Bakers met two English explorers, John Speke and James Grant. These men had already found the lake that was the main source of the Nile. They had named it Lake Victoria after the Queen of England.

Speke and Grant told the Bakers that there might be another lake. The unknown lake could be a source for the Nile, too. The Bakers decided to search for it.

The Nile

The Nile is the longest river in the world. It is more than 4,130 miles (6,650 kilometers) long.

People can only sail on 2,000 miles (3,200 kilometers) of the Nile. The rest is full of waterfalls and rapids.

Crocodiles, hippos, and other animals live in the Nile's water. Nile Perch live in the Nile, too. They often weigh over 200 pounds (90 kilograms).

Florence Baker once shot a charging rhinoceros to save her husband's life. His gun had failed.

Discovery

The Bakers found the other lake on March 14, 1864. They named it Lake Albert to honor Queen Victoria's husband, Prince Albert. The Bakers discovered that the Nile flowed out of two lakes, not just one.

The Bakers also discovered the largest waterfall on the Nile. They named it Murchison Falls to honor Sir Roderick

The Bakers met many African people while they explored the Lake Albert region.

Murchison. He was the president of the Royal Geographic Society in England.

Back to England
Finally, the Bakers went to London, England, in 1865. People treated Baker like a hero. He was honored for the discovery of Lake Albert.

They were surprised to see von Sass-Baker. No one knew that Baker had been married. People wondered about his mysterious new wife. Samuel made sure that Florence received credit for exploring.

Return to Africa

In 1870, the Bakers returned to Africa. They explored the Lake Albert region for three years. Von Sass-Baker kept records about the weather. She collected plants for scientific study.

The Bakers worked hard to make it against the law to sell or buy slaves in Africa. The king of Bunyoro put them in prison. They had to fight their way out of his capital city of Masindi to go home. They finally returned to England in 1873.

In later years, the Bakers journeyed to the American Rockies, to India, and to Japan. They never went back to Africa. Samuel Baker died in England in 1893. Florence von Sass-Baker lived until 1916.

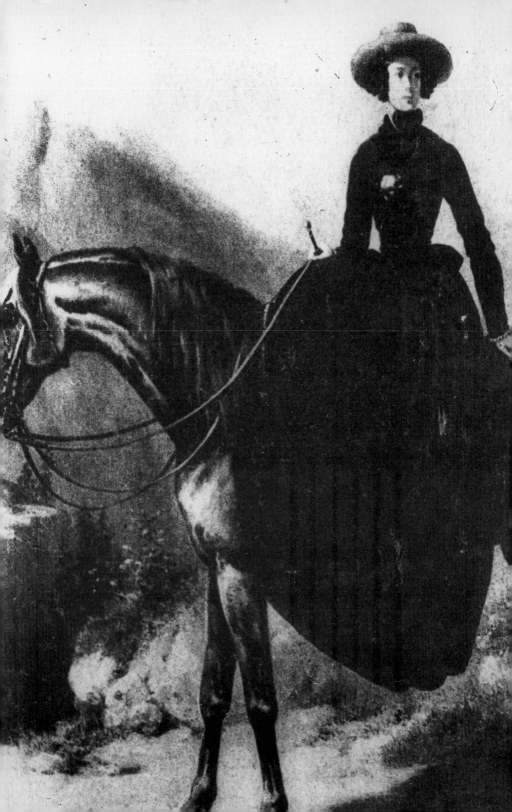

ALEXANDRINE TINNE 1835—1869

Alexandrine Tinne was born in The Hague, Netherlands, on October 17, 1835. Her parents were very rich. When Tinne was nine, her father died. She and her two brothers inherited his fortune.

Tinne learned many languages. She loved to travel. By the time she was a young woman,

Alexandrine Tinne could speak many languages.

she had visited most places in Europe. She decided to explore places on other continents.

Tinne heard about the mystery of the Nile. No one knew the river's source. She wanted to find it.

Journey on the Nile

In 1856, Tinne and her mother Harriet van Capellen-Tinne went to Cairo, Egypt. They rented a large boat to travel down the Nile. They stocked it with food, china, silver, furniture, and livestock. They hired maids, cooks, waiters, and secretaries.

After 10 weeks, they returned to Cairo and rented a house. Tinne had her piano shipped to Africa. She played music and planned another trip down the Nile.

Second Journey on the Nile

Tinne and her mother set out again from Cairo in January, 1862. On this trip, Tinne decided to go further into Africa. She was sure she could find the source of the Nile.

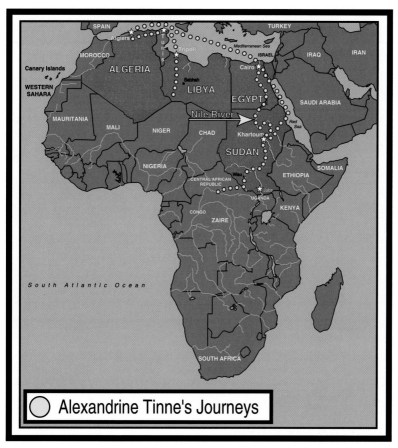

On the second trip, they took three boats. The Tinnes, their maids, and five pet dogs were on one boat. The other two boats were for servants, luggage, and livestock. In 12 weeks, they reached Khartoum, a city in the Sudan.

Alexandrine Tinne's body was never found.

Tinne hired many soldiers and scientists to help with her expedition. She left Khartoum with six boats. Tropical storms and illnesses ruined her search attempts. Her mother, her maids, a scientist, and her dogs died.

In January of 1864, Tinne returned to Khartoum. She gave up her search for the Nile's source.

Honored Explorer

Tinne lived and traveled in Africa for a few more years. She collected plant samples to send to a herbarium in Vienna, Austria. A herbarium is a place that keeps a collection of dried plants.

In 1869, Tinne set off across the Sahara Desert. She wanted to explore new routes to the middle of Africa. She had people make big iron tanks for her. She carried water in these tanks.

A fight broke out in Tinne's camp on August 1, 1869. One survivor said that an attacker chopped off Tinne's hand with his sword. She bled to death. She was only 34 years old. Her body was never found.

The survivors say that Tinne was killed by greedy desert tribesmen who wanted her money. The tribesmen thought that treasure was hidden in the iron tanks.

There is a stone monument in Juba, Sudan, that honors explorers of the Nile. Alexandrine Tinne's name is carved on that stone.

CHRONOLOGY

Alexandrine Tinne	Florence von Sass-Baker	Mary Kingsley
1835	**1841**	**1862**
Born in The Hague, Netherlands	Born in Transylvania, Romania	Born in London, England
1845	**1848**	**1888**
Tinne inherits family fortune	Family killed during Hungarian Revolution	Mary becomes her mother's nurse
1856	**1858**	**1892**
First journey on the river Nile	Samuel Baker buys Florence's freedom	Mother dies; father dies a few weeks later
1862—1864	**1861—1865**	**1893**
Second river Nile journey	Bakers explore Nile river areas in Africa	Takes first journey to West Africa
1869	**1870—1873**	**1895**
Sets out for the Sahara Desert	Bakers' second expedition to Africa	Takes second journey to West Africa
1869	**1916**	**1900**
Murdered in the Sahara Desert	Florence Baker dies in England	Dies in South Africa while nursing prisoners of war

Delia Akeley	Christina Dodwell
1875	**1951**
Born in Beaver Dam, Wisconsin, U.S.A.	Born in Nigeria, Africa
1902	**1957**
Marries Carl Akeley	Moved back to England
1905 & 1909	**1975**
Collects animals in Africa with Carl	Goes on trip to Africa; stays and explores
1924	**1984**
Becomes the first woman to lead a safari	Publishes *An Explorer's Handbook*
1929	
Leads a second expedition to Africa	
1970	
Dies in Florida at age 95	

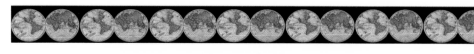

WORDS TO KNOW

artifact (ART-uh-fakt)—object that is made or changed by human beings and is usually used for a practical task

bush (BUSH)—a large wilderness area with little or no human settlement

cannibal (KAN-uh-buhl)—someone who eats human flesh

equator (i-KWAY-tur)—an imaginary line halfway between the North and South Poles; divides the earth into the Northern and Southern hemispheres

expedition (ek-spuh-DISH-uhn)—a trip taken by a group of people for a special purpose

herbarium (ur-BARE-ee-um)—a place for a collection of dried plants where sample plants are mounted, labeled, and used for scientific study

malaria (muh-LAIR-ee-uh)—a dangerous infection carried by mosquitoes; causes chills, fever, and sweating

Nile (NEYEL)—the longest river in Africa

Pygmy (PIG-mee)—a person who lives by the African equator whose height ranges between four and five feet (1 and 1-1/2 meters) tall

safari (suh-FAH-ree)—a journey for hunting or exploring, usually in Africa

Sahara (suh-HARE-uh)—the largest desert in the world; covers most of northern Africa

source (SORSS)—the place where a river or stream begins

TO LEARN MORE

National Geographic Society. *Exploring Your World: The Adventure of Geography.* Washington, D.C.: National Geographic Society, 1993.

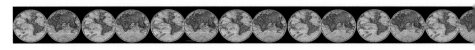

Rappaport, Doreen. *Living Dangerously: American Women Who Risked Their Lives for Adventure*. New York: HarperCollins, 1991.

Scheller, William. *The World's Greatest Explorers*. Minneapolis: The Oliver Press, 1992.

Stefoff, Rebecca. *Women of the World*. New York: Oxford University Press, 1992.

USEFUL ADDRESSES

National Geographic Society
1145 17th Street N.W.
Washington, D.C. 20036-4688

Royal Canadian Geographic Association
39 McArthur Avenue
Vanier, ON K1L8L7
Canada

Society of American Geographers
1710 16th Street N.W.
Washington, D.C. 20009

Society of Woman Geographers
415 East Capitol Street S.E.
Washington, D.C. 20003

INTERNET SITES

Earthwatch
http://www.earthwatch.org/

GlobaLearn
http://www.globalearn.org/

Mountain Travel Sobek: Adventure Company
http://www.mtsobek.com/

National Geographic Society
http://www.nationalgeographic.com/main.wd

INDEX

Akeley, Carl, 15, 16
Akeley, Delia, 15-19

Baker, Samuel, 31-35
Baker, Florence, 29, 31-35
Bambute, 16-19
Boer War, 27
bush, 10, 13

cannibals, 19, 21, 25, 26
Congo River, 11
Congo territory, 19
crocodiles, 11, 13, 26

Dodwell, Christina, 9-11, 13

elephant, 15, 18-19

Fang people, 25-26

Grant, James, 32

hippopotamus, 11, 26
Hungarian Revolution, 29

Jamieson, Leslie, 10
Kingsley, Charles, 23, 24
Kingsley, George, 23

Kingsley, Mary, 23-27

Lake Albert, 33, 35
Lake Victoria, 32
London, England, 9, 23

Milwaukee, Wisconsin, 15
Murchison Falls, 33

Nigeria, Africa, 9
Nile river, 31, 32, 33, 38, 40
Nile source, 31, 32, 38, 40

Ogowe River, 25

Sahara Desert, 10, 41
Simonstown, S. Africa, 27
Society
    Royal Geographic, 34
    Woman Geographers, 21
slave traders, 29, 31

Tinne, Alexandrine, 37-41
Tinne, Harriet, 38